# HOW LADY MET TRAMP

By ELLE STEPHENS

Based on the Screenplay by ANDREW BUJALSKI and KARI GRANLUND

Produced by BRIGHAM TAYLOR, p.g.a.

Directed by CHARLIE BEAN

LOS ANGELES • NEW YORK

For information address Disney Press,
1200 Grand Central Avenue, Glendale, California 91201.

Printed in the United States of America

First Paperback Edition, January 2020

1 3 5 7 9 10 8 6 4 2

FAC-029261-19343

Library of Congress Control Number: 2019949215

ISBN 978-1-368-05925-1

Visit disneybooks.com

One Christmas morning, a man named Jim Dear gave his wife, Darling, the best present ever: a puppy! She was a small, wriggly cocker spaniel.

"Jim Dear, she's perfect," said Darling. "A perfect little lady."

Every night after that, Lady slept in Jim Dear and Darling's bed, and she woke them up first thing in the morning.

Lady loved her home. She had a doggy door that she used to climb out into a big backyard. Most of all, she loved Jim Dear and Darling. And she knew they loved her, too. Every moment was perfect.

One day, Jim Dear and Darling gave Lady a very special gift: a shiny new collar with her name written on a gold heart.

Lady couldn't wait to show her friends Jock and Trusty, two dogs who lived in her neighborhood.

As she hurried out her doggy door, Lady spotted a rat! She chased it off the porch and told Trusty all about it. Trusty was a retired police bloodhound whose nose no longer picked up as many scents as it used to.

Just then, Jock arrived. She was a Scottish terrier whose owner always dressed her in snappy outfits. Jock immediately noticed Lady's new collar. "Must mean they really love you!" she told Lady.

One afternoon, Lady's house was full of people, including Darling's aunt Sarah. When she gave Darling a fancy vase, Lady jumped up to get a closer look.

"Careful!" shouted Aunt Sarah. "That dog needs to be trained."

Darling gently placed Lady on the floor. Confused, Lady crawled into the backyard. Through the fence, she told Trusty about what had happened.

"I know what your problem is," said someone on the other side—but it wasn't Trusty's voice. A stray dog named Tramp jumped over the fence and went into Lady's doghouse. He was hiding from a dogcatcher.

Once the dogcatcher left, Tramp explained why her family was acting so strangely: a baby was on the way. "You're about to be replaced," he said. Then he stole her bone and left.

When the baby arrived, things were very different.

One day, while Jim Dear and Darling were upstairs with the baby, Lady heard the rat again. She barked until Jim Dear came running, but then he put her out on the porch. Lady felt as if she couldn't do anything right.

A few days later, Aunt Sarah returned. She was to stay with Lady while Jim Dear and Darling took the baby on a trip. Soon after they left, Lady watched a pair of twin cats climb out of Aunt Sarah's basket. The cats looked at each other mischievously and then tore the house apart.

Horrified, Lady gave chase and barked for them to stop. But when Aunt Sarah saw the mess, she blamed Lady.

Aunt Sarah took Lady to a pet store to have a muzzle put on her. As the muzzle clicked shut, Lady panicked. She squirmed out of Aunt Sarah's grasp and ran into the street . . . then right into Tramp.

"I never thought I'd actually be happy to see you," she said.

Tramp looked at Lady's face. "I think I have a friend who can help you," he said. Tramp led Lady to a nearby park, where he cut off her muzzle using the teeth of a beaver statue. "So, baby moves in, dog moves out?" asked Tramp.

"It's not what it looks like," said Lady. She didn't want to admit to him—or herself—that maybe he had been right after all. She turned to leave but realized she didn't know how to get home.

"Follow me, kid," said Tramp.

TONY'S
RESTAURANT

Tramp showed Lady his favorite shortcuts. First they snuck aboard a riverboat. Then they hitched a ride on a horse-drawn carriage.

Then Tramp took Lady to his favorite spot: Tony's Restaurant, where Tony himself prepared a heaping plate of spaghetti and meatballs for them. Romance was in the air.

After dinner, Tramp told Lady that he once had a home, but his owners abandoned him.

Just then, a light shined on the dogs. It was the dogcatcher!

"Run!" said Tramp. The pair split up and ran as fast as they could, but the dogcatcher captured Lady. Tramp felt awful as he watched her get taken away to the pound.

Locked in a cage with a bunch of other dogs, Lady was terrified. But a pair of dogs named Peg and Bull tried to make her feel better.

"Nothing to worry about," said Peg. "You're adoptable." She said it as if other dogs—street dogs, like her and Bull—weren't wanted.

"But every dog should be adoptable," said Lady.

The next morning, the dogcatcher took Lady to the front office, where Jim Dear and Darling were waiting for her.

But Tramp had come to rescue her, too. He watched as Jim Dear and Darling hugged and kissed Lady all the way home. "They came for her," he said to himself, surprised.

Back at home, everything seemed to return to normal. Best of all, Lady got to know baby Lulu.

Lady told Trusty and Jock all about her adventures with Tramp. “Street dogs are just like us,” she said. “They just aren’t lucky enough to have homes.”

Lady did feel lucky—but something was missing.

That night, Lady was on the porch when Tramp came to see her. He wanted her to live with him.

"I belong here," said Lady, and Tramp left disappointed.

As Lady turned to go inside, she heard the rat—it was trying to climb in Lulu's window! Lady barked but Jim Dear and Darling were busy talking to the dogcatcher. Jim Dear put Lady in the pantry while the man insisted Tramp was very dangerous.

Tramp heard Lady barking and went back to help. She told him about the rat and he rushed upstairs to the nursery, where the rat was about to pounce! Tramp stopped the rat just in time.

Jim Dear and Darling heard the commotion and rushed upstairs. When they saw Tramp, they thought he had been trying to attack the baby.

"You're safe now," the dogcatcher told the couple, and he led Tramp away.

When Jim Dear finally let Lady out of the pantry, she raced upstairs and revealed the rat to Jim Dear and Darling. Then she ran out looking for Tramp.

With Jock and Trusty's help, she chased down the dogcatcher's wagon. The wagon toppled over, throwing Tramp into the street.

Just then, Jim Dear and Darling pulled up. They realized that Tramp had been trying to protect Lulu, not hurt her.

"Hold on!" called Darling.

"Ma'am, he's a street dog," said the dogcatcher.

"No, he's not," replied Darling. "He has a home." She held out her arms to Tramp, encouraging him to come to her.

Surprised and a little nervous, Tramp limped over to his new family.

And just like that, a street dog named Tramp became a rescue dog with a family of his own—and a brand-new shiny collar.

Lady was right: every dog should be adoptable, and every dog deserves a good home.